She...

A Trio of Short Fiction
Featuring Female Protagonists

by

Helen Claire Gould

Helen Claire Gould Books

To Amanda, hope you enjoy reading this as much as I enjoyed writing it.

Helen Claire Byrne.

☺

Also by Helen Claire Gould and available
from Helen Claire Gould Books:

Floodtide
The Stallion

First published in the UK in 2018 by
Helen Claire Gould Books,
Peterborough, Cambridgeshire.

ISBN: 978-0-9930812-4-8

Printed and bound in England in 2018 by
**4edge Limited, 22 Eldon Way Industrial Estate,
Hockley, Essex SS5 4AD**

Contents

The Rustling of Silver Fishes

The Rustling of Silver Fishes

Helen Claire Gould

LOOKING BACK, IT'S SO CLEAR NOW. Paddling in the stream was what changed Margy.

She'd never been an affectionate child, always adventurous, always wanting to run off and discover things. I knew from the time she refused to feed from me that there'd be problems. So I nursed my love for my daughter instead of nursing her.

They said in hospital that the bonding process would take longer because I'd had a Caesarean. "When you go through birth together, you can't help but bond with your baby, and she with you," they said. "But don't worry. It'll come."

It never did, not until Margy was eight and a half.

The stream bubbled with quicksilver fish that afternoon. I'd never seen so many in my life. They looked like plump whitebait. One of them caught my glance and held it, its stare resembling intelligence in its intensity. We took off our shoes and crept into the transparent water, not wanting to disturb the fish. Margy stepped further in than me, screwed up her face and gasped as if the sunlight had got in her eyes, or the water was too cold, and shouted, "Mum!"

"What?" I grinned back.

"The fishes are swimming around my legs. It doesn't half feel funny when they touch you."

"That's because they have scales instead of skin like we do."

Margy laughed.

A swan glided out from the reedbed at the bankside.

"D'you think this is Swan Lake?" Margy asked.

I grinned again. "It's a ballet, not a place."

"I know." She laughed again. We watched the swan busy itself among the reeds, head down. "What's it doing?"

"Let's have a look."

We paddled closer.

There among the reeds sprawled another swan, neck outstretched. Its mate had its head laid on it as if grieving. I glimpsed a flash of silver, and couldn't be sure where it was coming from.

"I think we'd better get out now," I said, fearing the water might be contaminated by the dead swan. We dried our feet on the grass, put our shoes back on and walked home. I'd learned not to try to cuddle her for fear of yet another rejection, so when we got home all I did was wash her down and dry her legs and feet with a towel.

"That's a nasty cut you've got on your leg," I observed.

"Doesn't hurt."

"D'you want a plaster on it?"

"Nnn-nope." As if to emphasise the point, she shook her head.

"Okay." I moved towards the bathroom door. "I'll get our tea."

"Okay."

Margy showed little interest in her food, and I wouldn't be eating until Gary got home, so I read the local paper. There wasn't much in it, just lots of adverts, a few motor accidents and another damn-fool company prosecuted for allowing genetically-altered wildlife to escape into the environment.

"We'd better get you ready for bed, young lady," I said.

"Mummy." Margy came up, put her arms around me, and climbed onto my knee.

"Are you sickening for something?" I enquired, raising one eyebrow and pursing my lips.

She smiled as if she were plotting something. They must

4

have been working on her even then.

But I couldn't resist her now that she was loving me at last. Eight years I'd waited for this.

She became more affectionate every day after that. Any opportunity she had she'd climb on my knee, stroke my face, or simply hold my hand. I suppose I should have realised something wasn't right, but I was drunk on affection, and besotted with this new Margy. I never resisted, not even when I noticed, about six weeks after Swan Lake, that her voice had changed.

"I don't feel well, Mummy," she said, and her voice echoed as if tinfoil were rustling in her throat.

It was the end of the summer holidays, and I suspected she didn't want to go back to school the following week. "You'll feel better when you've had some breakfast."

"No, Mummy, I mean I *really* don't feel very well."

"What's wrong? Is it a tummy-ache, or a headache?"

"Not really. It's a *sort-of* tummy-ache, but sort of not."

"Do you want to stay in bed until you feel ready to get up, then?"

Margy nodded. "Will you cuddle me to make me feel better?"

Thinking back, that was the last thing she herself ever said to me. "Of course." I took her on my knee and rocked her back and forth as if she were a baby again. How I'd longed to be able to do this before!

She didn't make a sound when I put her down and explained that I had to see Daddy off to work and would come back as soon as he'd left.

And when I came back, she was lying on the bed, just as I'd left her, head lolling like a drunkard's on the pillow. Her skin was translucent, glinting like the waters of a stream in moonlight.

I knew something was very wrong with my baby.

5

Yet she spoke. "I have to get close to you," she said. But her limbs flopped as if weak; she couldn't move, not even to hold her arms up to be lifted. And there was that queer rustling again, like silver paper in her throat.

I still couldn't resist her. "Come here, darling," I said. "Mummy loves you *so* much!"

She lay on the bed, not moving. "I have to get close to you," was all she said.

I made to gather her up in my arms, but a ripple of silver passed beneath her skin and brought a twist of nausea to my throat. I stepped back a pace, hoping I wasn't going to throw up.

"I have to get *close* to you!" This time that rustle contained a greater urgency; but it wasn't like *her* childish voice any more. And when I saw her eyes, I knew.

A vast hunger had emptied them of all emotion.

I understood then that she was really dead, and only the parasites she carried within her animated her. I dropped her like a broken doll, and the little silver fishes burst forth from every orifice, sprouting little reptilian legs and flying at me with jaws open.

No time to grieve. I turned and ran, slammed the door behind me, and fled down the stairs.

They followed me. Flapped under the door to get to me, ignoring the fact that they were breathing neat air.

I dared not stop to phone the doctor. I ran out of the house screaming. *That's not my baby any more.*

I ran to a neighbour's house. "Carol!" I shrieked, and thumped on the door.

She opened the door. But one look at the silver stream which had followed me across the road, and she screamed and slammed the door in my face.

I ran to the next house. There was no response, and now the fish flopped across the drive to it to block my escape. I felt the facing bricks of the garden wall grate against my hip, and climbed instinctively.

The fish made a silver carpet which squirmed back and forth below me. But they didn't ooze up the wall after me. *They can't climb,* I guessed. *At least, not yet.* A bough from the large oak tree near the wall nudged me and I grabbed at it and swung up onto it. *They* aren't *going to get me!*

The branch swung about under my weight, but I clung on. Not only was I safer up here, but I could also see into Carol's porch. She was on the phone, waving her arms around as she spoke. I guessed she was phoning the police.

Then I heard a rustling like silver paper below me and looked down.

The fish had swarmed up the tree trunk. The corrugated bark offered them grip. I realised that their malevolent intelligence had evolved at a ferocious rate. They weren't afraid of anything, and the first four feet of the trunk were silver with wriggling whitebait now.

I inched along the bough – until I realised that took me closer to the trunk. I stared around me, looking for somewhere safer to move to. Panic clogged my lungs. There was nowhere. All I could do was climb. I reached for the nearest branch to steady myself as I crept back along the limb I stood on. *I must keep away from the trunk,* was my one thought.

And then, I felt the heavy branch beneath my feet sway. *But I can't go too far.* I stretched out my arm to heave myself up onto that bough. The bark scraped my hands. Branch by branch, I pulled myself up and away from the horror beneath me. My skin was raw where it came into contact with the rough bark. My knees and hands stung and bled. And all the time the limbs flexed and swayed under my weight.

If I fall, they'll be waiting –

And as my blood soaked into the bark the silver whitebait below wriggled and squirmed like maggots. *They* must *be able to smell my blood. It excites them.*

Then I realised: I'm *their prey.*

I was perhaps ten or twelve more feet up when a vehicle's brakes screamed in the road below. Men jumped out, clad in white suits with helmets, shouldering backpacks.

They're going to fry the fish, I thought, and froze in alarm. *What if it sets fire to the tree?*

There were shouts, then streams of fire jetted at the ground. In a few seconds the smell of scorched fish reached my nostrils. I dared look down.

With a plop, a charred GM fish fell off the trunk. Then another, until all I could hear was the patter as they hit the seared ground.

"You can come down now, Mrs. Wensall," one of the men called. His voice sounded distorted through his protective helmet.

I was too afraid to move until some of the men got a ladder and climbed up to help me down. I was so glad of human contact I didn't notice, until my feet touched the ground, that the NetStar logo was on all the suits, with a little silver star trapped in the arc. Beneath it a motto read, "A BRIDGE TO THE FUTURE".

"More of the buggers must've got out than we realised," my rescuer said. "And they breed in a host. But you're safe now."

But he'd reminded me of Margy. "My baby," I sobbed. It came home to me then – I'd never see her again.

The men from NetStar searched the house before letting me go back in. They didn't let me see what was left of Margy. "You've had enough shocks for one day," the man who'd helped me down said.

Ah, to have my darling back, even as she was before! The silver fishes gave me the loving child I'd always wanted for a few short weeks – then took her away from me forever.

Gary and I have a court case pending, and they say we have a good chance of winning, in the circumstances. We have witnesses, although all the evidence was destroyed – of necessity.

But what good will that do? It won't bring Margy back to me. All I can do is nurse my love for her and remember how her eyes glittered with mischief when she was at her most tomboyish. She never would let me nurse her, even as a tiny baby.

I've never fancied whitebait since then, either.

Witchbabe

Helen Claire Gould

"THERE ARE A COUPLE OF OPTIONS you might like to consider," the doctor said.

Infertile?

I felt stunned. So I didn't really listen as she explained the options. I heard her voice droning on like background music. After everything I'd been through, the endless examinations, being poked and prodded in all the wrong places, I wasn't sure I wanted any more of the same. I nodded and watched her face, but couldn't really take in what she said. Finally she stopped speaking, and the impact of her last sentence sank in upon the sudden silence in the room.

"Come back and see me in a week's time when you've discussed it with your husband."

"Thank you, doctor. I – appreciate all the help you've given us." I got to my feet, feeling numb inside. I hardly heard her say, "That's all right," behind me as I reached for the door handle, missed, tried again, and stumbled into the corridor.

I realised as I groped towards escape that there were hardly any options. *If you discount IVF, that only leaves adoption or surrogacy.* A rare combination of circumstances had made me unable to conceive, while otherwise apparently normal. I couldn't produce a child for my husband, or even for myself. Those circumstances hadn't – couldn't –erase the longing to procreate.

The light in the corridor was that of a February afternoon. The walls looked grey in the gloom. I felt like a war zone refugee as I lurched towards the waiting room.

It was empty. I couldn't help feeling, with a part of me that wasn't numb and ruined, how fortunate it was that I'd been the last patient.

Infertile!

I was on autopilot as I made it through the door, into the lobby, and past reception. My unsteady feet carried me outside, stopping for nothing. It was that time of year when twilight approaches as slowly as a cripple, then night rushes in like a lunatic. The door closed with a faint click behind me.

I scanned the car park for my car. Everything looked grey, even the air; the mist blended sky into pallid ground. I had to put a hand out to the colourless brickwork of the Health Centre to support myself. Yes, there it was, the metallic grey-blue of the Astra. It almost blended with the dreary greyness that pervaded the car park. *I don't want to die without having had a child.*

And then I remembered. *I need to go to the pharmacy first.* I couldn't go home and shut myself away yet. I still had to pretend everything was normal. I had to hold back the tears that longed, like subtle entities, to be born.

"Damn periods!" I muttered as I turned away from the refuge of my familiar vehicle. *It's not even as if I'll ever get pregnant. It's my body mocking me. No wonder they call it the Curse!*

Anger gave me more purpose than I'd had a moment ago. I turned towards the shops. They looked as grey as the rest of the buildings. The afternoon light had faded fast.

There was a cry. I looked around. A flash of bright red materialised and hurtled towards me. Pain jabbed my foot. I screamed.

I heard a voice from a long way off. "Martin, look where you're going!"

I looked down. The blur of colour resolved itself into a toddler in a red coat. In the dim light he squinted up at me from a red trike. Irrationally I noticed the trike's pedals were bright yellow. As a child I'd had one just like his.

"I'm so sorry!" the woman rushed up and laid a hand on my arm. "I hope he didn't hurt you! He's only just got it, and he loves it, but he's not all that careful with his steering yet."

I stared at her. The happy pride in her voice taunted me. Her bright clothes and prettily-coloured complexion radiated light in the dusk, making me aware of my own lank hair and dingy skin. A sense of unreality disoriented me and hit me like a hammer blow as once more my awareness withdrew from my surroundings. Just as the dusk had washed colour out of the day, I longed to be erased with the light, and diffuse like smoke into the air. It was torture just to stand there between the woman and the child.

She chattered on, but I hardly heard her. It seemed to me that she spoke in a language I didn't know, and never would, know. So simple, yet so impossible. *Any old fool can get pregnant,* I'd told someone glibly, long ago. Well, this old fool couldn't. A sense of alienation settled around me. Her voice was so much noise in the damp still air.

INFERTILE!

I turned and limped to the car, leaving the girl mid-twitter, mid-sentence, to stare after me. There was a dull ache in my foot, but around my frozen heart, ice cracked with every step. *That* pain I felt. I crossed the service road. I'd forgotten my errand. I passed under the trees. They were bare of leaves. The twigs stretched, stiff and nondescript, into a gathering darkness, sterile of all but droplets of moisture.

I reached the refuge of the car and unlocked the door with fingers that shook so much I dropped the keys twice. Once inside I collapsed over the steering wheel. Then the tears came, and with them sobs of grief so hard that they unlocked all the feelings I'd refused to acknowledge before.

I don't want to die without having had a child. I longed

to give my husband a child, the ultimate gift, after myself. I knew it was impossible, but I still wanted it to happen. I felt cheated. *I want the feel of a child's silken skin next to mine. I want the status of motherhood.*

I knew how much my husband wanted our child, too.

"It's not fair," I whispered to myself. "She can't control her child, while I can't have one at all." I knew it was irrelevant that the woman couldn't control her child, but it seemed like a perfect and insulting irony to hang my grief on. I felt great guilt over my resentment, but couldn't deny it. "It's just not fair."

*

I never went back to see the doctor. I went to see the witch instead.

She didn't look like a witch the first time I met her. We'd got chatting in the second-hand bookshop, quite by chance, when I noticed that there was a large section of books on magic, and remarked on this to the proprietress. She smiled strangely, and I found myself telling her my difficulties a few moments later.

"Come and see me tonight," she said. "I might be able to help." Of course, I couldn't resist that. She told me the address. A knowing half-smile lingered about her lips.

When I arrived, in the middle of a virulent rainstorm, she was waiting for me. Half of me didn't want to enter the house, but the other half drove me on. She had dressed in a ragged black robe which fluttered around her ankles. She gave me bitter tea which did nothing to soothe my nerves, ragged ever since the visit to the Health Centre two weeks before. We talked for hours, it seemed, but afterwards I couldn't remember what we'd said. It seemed I was both aware and unaware – at the same time – of all that had passed between us.

"Come, then," she said, "the time approaches." And she flung open a door that led into no room at all.

At first I thought I'd step out over a void if I passed through that door. Then I saw the half-rotted fire escape that led up to the attic. Panic suddenly hit me. I draw back, a sharp movement. I couldn't help it. I didn't *want* to go out there. *How did I let her persuade me?* I asked myself, not once but several times.

"You've paid. You can't back out now," she said, a hint of malice curving her wrinkled lips, and this time, exposing sharp teeth. It was a moment before I realised what was so strange about her smile. Her teeth had been filed. I just had time to wonder if she got toothache from it before her shove propelled me outside.

Thunder crashed around our ears. Lightning strikes split the darkness. I'd always enjoyed storms before; a battle with nature itself held exhilaration for me. This time, though, apprehension replaced excitement as the gale approached. Shutters on windows swung, slammed, and then swung again. The witch turned to me and urged me on. Her ragged robes streamed at each gust, then fastened, soaked, back on her legs. We clung to the rickety handrail, fighting the blasts of frigid air. Rain surged down in sheets. The sky growled. I slipped on the planking once, and even when I regained my balance it yielded underfoot. Once, the witch yelled, "Come on!" at me through the clamour.

The wind threatened to pluck me from the fragile staircase several times. I climbed hand-over-hand to reach the top of the ladder. The witch wrenched open the attic door. Even through the chill dense arrows of rain, the smell was overpowering, as if strange things had been wrought there many times before. We fell inside. Though I was glad of the shelter, my fear of what would happen next was a hard knot in my stomach.

The witch yanked the door to behind us. I shrank back into the chair she indicated, wondering about her. How had she come to this vocation? I knew she lived alone in this house, which must crumble further every year. Perhaps she was also childless. *But in her case,* I thought, *it's from choice.*

As if sensing my curiosity, the witch spoke. "Rest. You'll need your energy later." I thought I detected irony in her voice. "I have…preparations to make."

I closed my eyes. I heard her move about, efficient, not one to waste effort. I felt as if I were living in a dream. There are many shades of reality.

At last she spoke again. "Ready?"

I nodded.

In the dimness of the attic, all was quiet. Either the storm had receded or I'd withdrawn into myself. The witch told me to concentrate and think only of what I wanted.

She'd drawn a circle on the floor. The brazier flared with a flame that had a black tinge at its heart. It was still a flame, not smoke. She'd lit candles, and they too flamed black. They guttered in the wind from the re-opened door and shutters. It was as if she wanted to invite all the wildness the storm had to offer right inside the room. The incense filled the air with a hot heavy reek. We were both naked. The witch chanted, words that were familiar without being so, a half-memory that teased the edge of my consciousness. I closed my eyes again. The atmosphere in the room was sullen as we awaited whatever would happen.

And after several moments, something did. First, I became aware that the witch's chanting had ceased. Then I felt someone – or something –watched me. But not from inside the circle, where I expected it to be. The witch stood there. She'd drawn the circle to protect *herself,* not to chain the thing she'd summoned.

It was small, yet on a level with me. As I watched it flowed, changed, grew, and in a way I couldn't comprehend. When I rubbed my eyes and looked again, it had solidified into a diminutive man who stood on an onyx table nearby.

His eyes were a blue so bright as to be almost turquoise, and so piercing as to be able to see into my soul. He looked ancient and youthful at the same time. Deep lines ran across his forehead. Yet he was the size of a child about seven.

"I see you want something of me," he observed in a voice as gentle as the touch of silk. "Lift me."

I lifted him into my arms, resting him on my hip, as I would have lifted the child I longed for. He clung to my body. He swelled with the obscene fecundity of a chemical garden. His trunk was now the size of a man's. There was something ghastly about his dimensions. Disproportionate. Now he didn't seem so childlike...I felt a firm lump pressing against my hip. I grew frightened. For a moment I stared into his face, seeing the wrinkled skin and knowing I was about to transgress against nature.

That I should be brought to this...

"You cannot undo what you have begun," he said. I thought he must be reading my thoughts as they occurred to me. At this evidence of his power I grew still more frightened. I tried to let go of him, to put him down, but although my hands flailed wildly in the smoke-filled air, still he clung, not using his foreshortened limbs, just hanging there against me like a leech, as if defying gravity.

He spoke again, in that voice like the subtle caress of silk, and gestured at the same time. "Come, lie with me." With him still attached to my shrinking flesh, I climbed on that onyx table. My hands were so moist that I couldn't grip the slick surface, and I nearly slipped. I thought he'd suck the heart out of me, drain it dry and discard it.

"Oh no," he said. Now his voice was silk smeared with honey. "That's not the bargain – it's for something else..."

When the thing was done I was frantic to escape. It hadn't been pleasure, as it was with my husband. I supposed it wasn't meant to be.

I remember nothing more, except the overwhelming terror that gripped me as I pulled the door of the attic shut behind me and climbed out on that rickety fire escape again. The storm had rumbled away into the distance, but the rain still fell like arrows to pierce my fragile skin. At least the act was done and over with; what had been wrought there, no man or woman could now take away from me. I was whole at last, but filled with such terror that I struggled to shut the door on that thing I had called down on myself. I felt defiled. *Realising my dreams might yet cost me my sanity.* How could I bear to live with myself, I who had done this unnatural thing?

But for almost eight years, I did, not realising that while my son grew and played, a greater consciousness than I could even comprehend played with *me*.

*

It was his seventh birthday today. He sat in silence and watched all his playmates amuse themselves with the toys we'd bought for him. He hadn't joined in at all. At times I was surprised to see a sneer on his face, as if he was too clever to play like a child. Of course, he'd always seemed older for his age, but…

Yes, I'm a mother, but I'm never sure if *this* is how it's supposed to be. My husband looks confused sometimes as well, and I know just what he's thinking. He's not sure if this is what fatherhood's about, either.

The other kids have all gone home now. I spot an abandoned pink cardigan on the sofa. *Jennifer's,* my memory tells me.

I turn as I hear a choked cry from my husband. My son is nowhere to be seen.

"How…?"

He lies at my feet, the one I went through all this for. I can't bear to remember the suffering I endured to give him our child. He knew nothing of it. I kept quiet to save him pain. He thought a miracle had occurred at last. I know he'd have forbidden it if he'd known.

I kneel beside him, crooning to him as if *he* were my child. He can't hear me. His stomach has been slashed open. His blood congeals in the interstices of the carpet pile.

I become aware of my son watching me. It's as if I've looked at him, but never really *seen* him before. Bright turquoise eyes, piercing as if they can see into my soul. Ancient and youthful at the same time. Centuries old, seven years old.

Blood drips from his little hands. I stare at him. I feel sick as comprehension dawns.

"You left too soon," he says. "We hadn't discussed the price."

I was scared. I can't admit it, least of all to him. Still I stare. It isn't just the nausea, it's that I don't know what to say. Since I've realised why he did it, I can't utter the words, though I know what they are. At last I stutter, "Why did you have to take *him*? You had my body. That's a sacrifice from an otherwise faithful wife".

"That's not enough, not for a demon," he answers. "A woman's body is a paltry thing – a piece of mere machinery. There has to be a price."

Of course! He's so clever, giving what his victims want first, so that when he names his price they can't refuse him. And: *A woman's body isn't a paltry thing to her.*

The word *appalled* filters into my mind on a subliminal level. It's followed by *self-hatred* and *disgust*. I cannot speak.

"I'm going now," he says. His voice reminds me of the rasp of acid silk across bare skin. "You've had what you wanted from me. Now I've evened things up a bit. See you in hell...mother."

When I can bear to look again, he's gone.

There's a ring at the doorbell. A woman stands there. Her face is pleasant, smiling, as she speaks. "Jennifer was so excited she forgot her cardigan. I've come back for it."

She looks past me to the slumped, bloodstained figure on the hall floor. I don't know what to do. I move numbly aside as she enters, drawn by the body. Fascinated. Terrified.

Jennifer's mother has her mobile phone out. She speaks into it as the images skip through my mind. I've blocked them for almost eight years, and would rather forget them. They torture me with the memory of what I did for and to my husband, all without his knowledge. I never believed in adultery. *Especially not like that.* At the time I thought it was the only way to achieve my desire to be a mother. *All I wanted was to be like other women...*

Sirens wail, lights flash, I sit still, as if in a dream. I cannot leave. The police are here. Accusation stares out of their faces at me. "Where's the boy?" they ask many times.

"I don't know," I answer. "Why do you keep on asking me? I don't *know!*"

One of the policemen uses the radio. I hear a one-sided conversation. "The child may be in danger," he says.

Fools! I think. I haven't the will to struggle to speak the truth. An ancient compulsion warns me back from the abyss. I'm not sure if it represents salvation or damnation. My lips remain sealed, against all hope, all compassion.

Sudden insight focuses my mind on my son. The son that never was. At once innocent and guilty. A shout bursts forth from me. Meaningless. I feel froth accompany it, at the side of my mouth. I rush at one of the policemen, trying to punish him.

But it's *my* mistake. *I should have just accepted my allotted fate from God.*

I see the white shape of the ambulance draw up outside the house. More strangers enter. As they envelop me in a garment that binds my arms around my body in a vile hug, I

think of an onyx table in an attic room. My sacrifice.
  That I should be brought to this…

Spindrift on the Seas of Time

Spindrift on the Seas of Time

Helen Claire Gould

MY IMPRESSION IS AGAIN VERTIGO: I tumble head over heels relative to – nothing. Lights flash like shards of coloured glass. Acid burns my eyes, recoil stings my skin. I'm shattered like pottery, torn from end to end, side to side, inside out. Halved, quartered, fractionalised, fragmented, splintered, refracted –

With every trip I've felt pain and disorientation. I open eyes shuttered against dazzle. My mind moves in slow motion; around me everything moves too quickly, like double vision. Has the displacement stopped? Not yet.

At last the two tempos flow together and mesh. The madness ends – until next time.

Forgive me for leaving, Mother. I didn't want *to go. But Alia said I'd learn to control where and when I went, and that I could help you. You'd been in a coma for two days: the penultimate stage of Moroccan Fever. You were sinking fast. There was no time for goodbye.*

The grey light resolves into order; I've arrived where none can see me. Other physical sensations replace the pain: being in my body; blades of grass tickle my bare feet. The air I inhale tastes like wine. *No pollution.* It flows into my lungs like a river of rich, ripe scents.

I find an old robe and drape it toga-wise around me. In the distance, the slap of feet on the ground, speech, meetings. *But until I've done this for you, my life is not my own.*

Rough-hewn stone streets lead me into the town. Villas surround me. As I advance they crowd together and loom over me. I feel trapped.

A figure approaches. Hair dangles over its eyes and face. Its robes are dirty and torn, like mine. Its greige hair hides its eyes. The exposed remains of breasts cling, leech-like, to a concave chest; that tells me its sex. Her bare feet are dirty.

"You!" she shrieks as we pass each other. "You don't belong here!"

Panic swings my equilibrium in a dozen directions at once. *How does she know?* Then I remember my meeting with Alia, and understand. "Where is this place?" I ask.

"Why, Rome, of course!" Her voice creaks like cracked leather. She inspects me; I wilt under her impenetrable gaze. "You will not cheat death, nor will she to whom you seek to give life. You can only avoid it for so long." She walks on.

She's lost interest in me. I stare after her. *Will this whole journey be in vain? Is that what she means? Is there no cure for the Fever? But how would she know?*

And then: *Rome? That wasn't my destination.*

I try again. A wrenching shift sideways. Colours glow and sear the darkness. A giant's hand stirs the trans-dimensional broth and shakes me apart. The pieces fit back together at last, with subtly wrong reconstruction. My sense of being drifts free. I am mutable, mutable…mutable. Razors tear my skin. Kettledrums thunder in my head. Time impels me forwards and squeezes air from my lungs.

My feet touch the ground; I'm naked again. Alia warned me about that. This time I lurch to my feet before the world has stopped its orbit of my head. Before I can reclaim my balance there's a huge percussion nearby. *Where am I? A minefield?*

A tangle snares my skin. "Barbed wire!" The blood congeals almost at once. I react instinctively to the danger. I trip again, before they can report a nude female on the

28

battlefield. The thought of injury terrifies me as much as dying of the Fever does.

Once more the dislocation. *I will continue to improve each time.* The last day and a half have seen me trip up to two hundred times. My memories are awhirl with places and times. But the displacement wearies me mentally and physically. But I remember Alia's words before this mad journey: "Use your memory and imagination. *See* where you want to go. It makes it easier to get there."

I form a mental image this time. Perceptions transposed, I hold my breath. Blurs of colour swim around me. Neons illuminate the ether. Doubt assails me, despite my determination to take control. Rabid images mortify my flesh and emotions. I fall. Turmoil grows in proportion to my panic. I reach for anything to stop or slow the fall. There's nothing there. *How can there be? Surely Alia was a figment of my imagination?*

My bones ache. I'm desperate, lost, exposed; ravaged by time itself. *Where will I end up* this *time?* Thoughts navigate my mind and body, my companions in this dream of places that once existed, or will exist. *Will I ever rest again?* I know fear, and it knows me. It's too much to comprehend, let alone control.

*

I met Alia in a coffee bar.

She slipped into the chair opposite as I raised my cup. "May I join you?"

Her accent made me look up, distracted as I tried to place it.

"Dani Caxton?" she asked.

I shook my head. "That's my mother. But she's –" I couldn't bring myself to say the word. It sounded so final.

"Then – you're *Dori*?"

I nodded.

A frown rippled across her features, then disappeared, as if she'd filed away a thought for future exploration. "Can I just check something in your newspaper?"

It lay unread at my elbow. I pushed it towards her.

She scanned the front page, frowned again, then passed it back. "Thanks."

I acknowledged that with a slight nod. I resented the intrusion, but my curiosity was aroused as well. For the first time, I examined her. She seemed like any other woman with her cropped dark hair and putty-coloured trenchmac, but there was something foreign about her. It wasn't just the accent, but I couldn't analyse it then. "Perhaps you don't know me as well as you think." My voice was edged with irony.

"Then I'm falling down on my job." She spread her hands and frowned again as she studied me. "You're right. There are gaps in my knowledge. I hoped you could help me."

"What do you mean?" I was getting annoyed now. "Look. My mother is dying." There, I'd said it. It felt like I'd admitted it to myself for the first time. "There's no cure for her illness. I've got a lot to cope with right now, and I don't need hassle from people like you. Anyway, what are you – a Secret Service recruiter?"

She laughed. "Flatterer!" Her eyes and voice became serious. "I'm a Caxtan Temporal."

"A what?" I didn't know whether to be astounded or annoyed that someone thought fit to take me for a ride under the current circumstances.

"Let me explain."

"I think you'd better!"

"You're right. We're a secret organisation, and we provide a service, though not so's you'd notice." She stroked her coffee cup handle, unsure where to start, and drew in a deep breath. "We're an elite sect from the future."

I got up to go. "Don't take the piss! I've got enough on my plate right now. I don't need a stranger who speaks in puzzles and pretends to be something she couldn't be." I reached for my handbag.

She caught my wrist. "Sit down and be quiet." She stared into my eyes. "We need each other."

"What can you *possibly* have that *I* want?" Rage thudded in my veins, against her, against my mother for being ill, but most of all, against myself for letting this situation develop. My thoughts performed a mental somersault. "Oh, I get it," I said. "It's not about what *I* want. *You* want something from *me*."

She had the grace to bite her lip and nod. "It's vital that Dani survive."

"Because of her research to help sick people? How can that be of interest to a secret organisation?" Against my will my interest stirred. "Unless Morocco Fever was a terrorist invention, and you really *are* the Secret Service!"

She laughed and pulled my wrist to make me sit down. "We're not. Among other things, we research time cusps – important points in history where there's doubt as to what really happened. Dani's disappearance is one, though it seems certain now that she died of Morocco fever. She's also the founder of a sect that won't exist for another thirty-eight years. Without her research, millions will die – but to us the founding of our sect is even more important." She gestured towards windows streaked inside with condensation and outside with rain. "It's a filthy night out there. Instead of rushing off and getting soaked, why not just listen to me and make up your own mind about this?"

Grudgingly, I relaxed back into my seat.

She ordered more coffee.

"I hope you're paying for this," I said.

She smiled. "Coffee's one of the things I like most about researching this time period," she said. "My name is Alia."

"Riiiight. And you're a Caxtan Temporal. Whatever that is."

She shot me a warning glance from beneath lowered lashes. I looked round to see the waitress approach with a tray.

"I will explain," Alia promised softly. "And don't think I'm not sorry about your mother's illness. I am. I want to help." She waited till the waitress had gone again before adding, "It's essential you let me help."

"How can *you* help *me*?" I demanded, rage still bristling inside me. "You're the one with the doubt as to what happened to my mother."

"All because I know a different side of the story from the one you know –"

"Well, you would, wouldn't you, being from the future!"

"Calm down and listen." She paused to sip her coffee. "I'm working for the equivalent of what you call a thesis. Vital files have been lost. I'm here to investigate and fill in the gaps in our knowledge. Instead, I've discovered another mystery. You."

"If that's a joke it's not very funny," I complained.

"Later I'll show you something that proves I'm not joking," Alia said. "We Temporals ride the timelines, researching anomalies – time cusps – for historical reasons. More than that, we police time itself, without interfering in the past." She spoke about her sect with a passion that told me she, at least, believed what she was doing was real.

I've always considered myself a truthful person, and respect that quality in others. I began to warm to her. "So…where does my mother fit into all of this?"

"I've discovered from my research that she was working on a cure for Morocco Fever, but became ill with it herself," Alia said.

"Correct."

"What's the origin of this disease?"

32

I shrugged. "Nobody knows. In the past twenty years food supplies have dwindled in many countries. Some say the spate of new diseases evolved to reduce the population. There were terrible Food Wars in Africa and Asia – fertile ground for these diseases to develop.

"And Mother worked herself to the bone in search of a cure. Four weeks ago she was sure she was on the brink of discovery – then suddenly, she'd caught it herself. I've spent the last month watching her waste away. I can't even touch her. She's in a plastic isolation tent." I bit my lip. "Tonight, she told me she only has a few more days. Not that the doctors had told her; she knew enough about the fever to work it out herself. Not long after that she slipped into a coma."

"We don't know what the cure is, but we know someone found one," Alia said. "Perhaps it was you?"

"Have a heart – my mother's dying! I can't leave her just now."

Alia continued as if I hadn't spoken. "This is my assigned time period, so I can't leave it for long enough to search, but I could at least teach you how to trip. We could ask your mother what she was working on –"

"Didn't you hear what I just said? My mother's in a coma!"

"Ah…That might be difficult, then. But *you* could find the cure and prepare it –"

"Aren't you forgetting something?"

"What?"

"I'm not a biochemist. I've had no formal scientific training at all –"

Alia stared at me. "I didn't know that." She shook her head. "Some things don't fit at all…" she mused. Then she spread her hands. "It doesn't matter. Your mother's associates will know how to prepare the cure, once they know what it is."

"Are you sure about that? Mother's work is pretty experimental. All I know is that it's based on plant-derived compounds."

"They'll know," Alia murmured. Confidence and satisfaction filled her voice. I supposed that she'd found out what she wanted to know and got me to agree to her demands.

It was late when I followed Alia into the deserted streets. The sky rolled black and thunderous above our heads, pierced by the rooftops of buildings that lined the pavements. A wave of premonition washed over me. "It feels like I'm on an avenue that leads straight to hell."

"In a way, you are," Alia said, looking around. "Ah – this will do."

It was darker and wetter than ever in the alley she stepped into. I looked up. The walls curved together above our heads. I shivered and followed Alia.

"Come on!" she hissed, and grabbed my arm, pulling me further into the darkness. "Now hold tight."

And as the walls twined together overhead, the clouds snaked between them and plucked at the very fabric of my being. I could feel my body being shaken apart, then cut into slivers, each of which knew the destruction going on inside it. But through it all, Alia's grip on me was still there, as I breathed icicles, pissed splinters of glass, and bled fire.

I thought it went on for ever. Once I heard her say, from close by, "It's a little disorienting when you trip." I didn't think to reply that she could say that again; I'd forgotten how to speak. I concentrated on retaining a semblance of continuity to my existence. She was probably just used to it.

There came a thunderclap that sounded as if the universe had split in two. A shaft of lightning burst against my tortured eyeballs, and the mind-wrenching ceased. It was still dark.

"Sorry about that," Alia said. "It's always worse when you cross a timeline."

I blinked. "So what do you do for fun?"

Alia smiled that secret smile of hers again, but kept hold of me. "Walk with me," she said. "And remember – we *must* keep physical contact, whatever happens."

"Why?"

"Because I'm your passport back to your own timeline. If we get separated you'll be trapped here. I'll teach you how to trip when we get back."

"Why can't you teach me now?"

"It's not a good idea to learn to trip in a different timeline." She hauled on my arm. "This way." After a moment she added, "Anyway, I want to show you this first. It's *a* future, but not yours – if you do as I say."

I dawdled despite the chill air. The deserted streets glistened with recent rainfall. I relaxed, until I realised we were both naked as newborns. "Don't we need some clothes?"

Alia looked at me meaningfully, but a mild, "If and when we can get some," was all she said.

We stepped out into the main street. In the distance I heard shouting or movement. Alia steered us both around piles of rubbish, broken glass, and dog shit. I was grateful for her pilotage. Without it I'd have blundered into something. My reeling mind still hadn't settled.

The noise got louder. Closer.

"We'll hide in here," Alia said, "and get some clothes while we're about it." She dragged me through a shop doorway. The windows were cracked; one door hung at a crazy angle. She walked straight through. That summed her up neatly: a woman who knew where she was going and let nothing get in her way. Perforce, I had to follow as she helped herself to a jacket, trousers, and shoes. "Get some stuff!" she ordered. She pulled the clothes on, and changed her grip on me as necessary.

I obeyed, partly from fear. I could hear the stomp-stomp of feet beneath the shouts now.

"Get down, watch, and keep quiet. Don't let anyone see you, or we're done for!"

We crammed ourselves between a carousel of coats and the shop window, where mannequins paraded and pirouetted in ripped and faded clothes in a static ballet. No-one had bought clothes here for a long time.

I heard the wheeze of lungs bursting for breath before a man's figure limped into view. He shuffled along, his exhaustion clear.

The noise of feet and shouting grew. The pursuers burst into the street, all wasted faces and flesh that dribbled and pouched over distorted bones. Their eyes were mad with a hunger from which there was no escape.

I knew that look. My mother had it now. "They've all got Morocco Fever!" I whispered.

"Yes. But in *this* future, there is only one cure." Alia shook her head. "To steal the body of a healthy person."

"How do they do that?"

"They trip. Simple as that. An ex-Temporal outlaw named Cassandra taught them. But they just spread the disease."

Something occurred to me. "I think I met her in Rome."

"You saw her?"

"Old, grey hair, scrawny, shrieky-creaky voice?"

Alia nodded. "That's her all right. And she has to be stopped –"

The lead man stumbled as a missile hit him fair and square in the centre of his back.

"Won't he get it too?"

A nod. "And the crowd could tear him to pieces in the rush to take his body. Shush!"

The crowd was level with our refuge. The street was full, but the shouting faded as the man disappeared under the crowd. I couldn't see what was happening for the press of people. Someone screamed – perhaps the prey had fallen on some glass. I grimaced. After the horror of the cross-dimensional trip I felt the imagined injury as if it were my own.

"We'll wait till they've gone, then go back to your timeline," Alia murmured. I could only nod my assent.

The marchers piled on past, some seeking another prey, some still walking because there was nowhere else to go.

*

The sound of boots had faded before Alia pulled me upright and we ventured outside.

"H-help me..."

A man lay against the broken window of the shop next door, covered in blood and vomit.

I stepped forward.

Alia pulled me back. "Don't be a fool! You can't help him without becoming sick yourself. Everyone dies here – it's where Morocco Fever started, and Cassandra spread it. Your own timeline needs *you* to find the cure. Now let's get out of here."

Even after what I'd seen, the prospect of another sidewise trip through time was daunting. I drew a deep breath as Alia led me down a side street.

"It shouldn't be as bad this time," she said.

I still think she was either joking or mistaken.

Once back on solid ground, we found our clothes again.

"We've got a busy night ahead. I'll teach you to trip. Then you can find out what your mother needs for the cure." Alia told me a bit about it. "Try for the rainforest. The native people there may know of something, and biodiversity is greater in the tropics. If necessary, go into the past. There's no time to lose."

I stared at her in dismay. My limbs felt like lead, which I suppose wasn't too bad for someone who'd time-tripped twice in the last forty minutes. "Actually I'd like some sleep first. I learn better if I'm not tired."

"Time's at a premium."

"So's sleep. Anyway, can't you just arrive back at the same point in time that you left from?"

"If you've learned that degree of fine control."

"Well, whatever, I'm not going anywhere until I've slept." I argued with her until I got my way, though it was only common sense. I became intimately acquainted with alleys I'd never realised existed as we trudged back to my flat.

I made her more coffee and yawned.

Even Alia shivered in the warmer atmosphere inside. "You can sleep till daybreak. I'll teach you to trip at first light. And you'll just have to keep jumping until you find out what the cure is."

"And then keep jumping again till I find my way back?"

"That's it exactly."

*

Surrounded by the tallest trees I've ever seen, I peer around. The understory is higher than my head and thickly foliated, but not continuous. The isolation of this tiny pocket of forest is complete. I listen for a moment to the sounds around me: the chirp of tree-frogs, birdsong, the drone of insects…and a rustle as the leaves of a bush part.

"Who – who's there?" I call.

A young woman steps from behind the bush. She carries a basket and wears a stained camouflage-effect shirt and khaki shorts with her boots and socks. "My name is Felipa," she says. "Can I – er – help you?"

I look down at my naked body. Whether she can help with some spare clothes depends on how long I stay, but I realise I've acquired some of Alia's *sang-froid* regarding nudity. "Perhaps. Are you – um –" Now that I'm here, it seems rude to ask someone I've only just met if they belong to a rainforest tribe. I take a deep breath and start again. "I'm looking for anyone from a rainforest tribe."

Felipa smiles. "I'm a botany student on a field trip but I know some of the tribes here. Actually there are only a couple of tribes left in this part of the forest. I can take you to meet them if you like."

"That would be helpful. I need to speak with a shaman or –" here I hesitate, unsure how to pronounce the word – "*vegetalista*."

"Why?"

I look into her basket. It contains a collection of berries and leaves. I decide it's worth confiding in her. "I'm here to try to find a cure for Morocco Fever. There's probably a vegetable compound that would work, and the *vegetalistas* know about stuff like that."

Felipa frowns. "There aren't any shamans around now, and the *vegetalistas* died out in this area in the 1950s."

"Oh dear...that's bad news!" I sigh. *Perhaps I should go back to the 1950s, but that was at least 80 years ago now.*

"But it sounds as if we have a common interest in these *vegetalistas*." I listen carefully. She pronounces the word with a soft 'zh' sound instead of a harder 'j' sound, and the stress falls on the penultimate syllable. "Apparently a dispute split the group...*I* want to rediscover their knowledge about the local rainforest plants and their properties for *my* dissertation. Why don't you come and join us students? We might be able to help a bit, and it'll get dark soon. I invite you to dinner, such as it is!"

I look up, and see that she's right. The fragments of sky visible through the tree canopy are a darker blue than when I arrived. I'm hungry and naked, and it makes perfect sense to accept. I've been tripping for at least a full day.

Felipa finds me a spare shirt and shorts, and I'm grateful for the supper of casseroled beans and herbs. I'm even more grateful for the chit-chat about who's discovered what, as darkness cloaks the forest and its sounds become even more noticeable against the stillness. One group have found a family of plants that cause paralysis, and eventually death; but they think they'll be useful for anaesthetics; Felipa's group have discovered berries and leaves that, if cooked down, yield a mush with the potential to protect against heart disease. And another group are investigating what happens when mushroom-like growths on the forest floor are combined with the berries. I file all my observations away for future use, and curl up on the floor to rest my aching body as quietness falls in the students' camp.

The next morning I leave. I return the clothes to Felipa, with a note containing my thanks, and set off to find a quiet corner of the forest where I can trip back to the 1950s.

*

For once, I've arrived just where I want to – or right overhead. A flurry of foliage greets my entry into the 1950s rainforest. I soon realise why: I visualised the canopy. As I fall earthwards I grab at branches to slow my progress. I acquire many scratches in the process.

I hear more than one crack under my weight.

But it strikes me: *I really have achieved a degree of fine control.* I feel a hint of pride as I step naked into a clearing at ground level. In the sunlight I see scratches on my arms and legs.

Apes screech and chatter above and I hear them leap from tree to tree in the canopy. I hear a loud crack far above and look up.

And out of the corner of my eye, I see him – at the same instant – a young man runs towards me. He waves his arms and yells, "Look out!"

Although I don't speak Portuguese, I do know a little Spanish, and by instinct I turn and look upwards again. I see what he's noticed.

A large branch falls through the canopy. It catches on others on the way down as it heads straight for me. I realise I probably broke it on my way down.

I can't move. I'm torn between the need to trip away from danger, and the desire to stay now I'm here. I can't process both needs at once.

The next second, the man's on me. His impetus rolls us over a couple of times on the forest floor.

With a crash not softened by the swish of foliage, the bough lands nearby at the same time, followed by two or three smaller ones.

I register pain in the hip and shoulder that hit the floor as I sit up. But I'm alive and functional for my task. "I think you just saved my life," I say. "Thank you!"

"No problem, lady," he says, in accented English. I study him for a moment. He wears a t-shirt, shorts, boots and socks, just like Felipa and her friends. *The uniform hasn't changed then,* I think. He seems a lot like Felipa and her student friends. "But where are your clothes? You need them for protection in the jungle."

"I don't have any with me." And as we climb upright I become fully aware of my nudity. I lay an arm across my breasts, and place my free hand over my most private parts. At the same time, I remark the sting of scraped skin and the dull pain a couple of bruises bring, and wince.

"Are you hurt?" he asks, his brown eyes anxious. "I'm so sorry, I didn't mean to injure you –"

"Nothing serious," I say.

He doesn't seem the least bit fazed by the fact that I'm naked; but perhaps he thinks I feel threatened, for he says, "Don't worry, I'm not going to attack you."

In truth I feel more self-conscious than threatened. It seems obvious to me that he won't attack me, or he wouldn't have saved me.

"I didn't really think about it – I just did the first thing that came into my head." He steps back from me and checks me over as a medic would. "You have a couple of nasty bruises on your hip and shoulder. I can fix those. I have something for your scratches too. Come with me."

I follow him to a hut in a clearing in the forest, arm and hand still in place. It has a more European-looking construction than I expect, with a door and a large window.

"In here," he says, as he brandishes a key and unlocks the door. "This is my surgery."

And then, as we enter the hut, I realise why he came over as caring rather than threatening.

Inside, rows of shelves stacked with jars cling to three walls. A large, old-fashioned mirror occupies almost all of one wall. I'm struck by its ornate, gilded frame. A glass window occupies the fourth wall, below which stretches a bench of some native wood, on which lie many unidentifiable pieces of equipment. Most are made of glass and look scientific in nature. One thing I do recognise: a pestle and mortar.

"It's like an apothecary's shop in here," I say.

He smiles as he reaches for a jar, then offers it to me. "That's exactly what it is, I suppose. Rub some of this salve on your hip and shoulder." He passes me a second jar when I've done so. "Now wash your hands here –" he indicates a bowl under a tap protruding from an old-fashioned wooden barrel on the worktop, and a towel on a hook nearby "– and put some of this on your scratches. Then wash your hands again afterwards. There's the soap."

I obey, wondering if this is the man I've come back in time to meet as I wash my hands again.

"I'm Ramo, by the way," he adds. "I conduct my research and consultations in here."

"I'm Dori Caxton."

We shake hands.

*

I sit watching Ramo as a trickle of people come in for one treatment or another throughout the day. He has a pleasant manner with everyone. He knows them all by name, listens attentively to their ills, and smiles as he remembers the last time they came to him. He asks one woman how her father is, having treated him recently.

Apparently, he's much better, thanks to Ramo's medicine.

"Coffee?" he asks me.

"Thank you, that'll be lovely." I hitch up the spare pair of shorts he's found for me, and flap the spare t-shirt to fan my heated skin. "How come you have this place?"

"A German doctor came to the tribe about twenty-five years ago and practiced medicine here. This hut was his."

"Where did you get your gorgeous mirror?"

"My mother brought it with her from her family's house in Rio when she married my father."

"It's very ornate," I observe, "but beautiful and stylish in its own way."

"My mother was from a good Portuguese family, and my father was the tribal chief's son."

"Does that mean the chief of the village is your father now?" I ask.

"Yes. But my mother died a few years ago."

I'll ask him about Morocco fever, I resolve. *He may know nothing, but he seems like just the right man to ask.*

And later, I think of how Ramo helped the woman's father, and it gives me the confidence to ask, "Ramo, are you a shaman, or a *vegetalista*?"

He smiles. "A little of both, I think. I'm an unofficial doctor."

I explain about my mother, her work, and my quest. The only thing I don't tell him is that I'm from the future.

"Why do they call it Morocco Fever?" he asks.

"My mother said that's where the first cases appeared."

"OK, that fits." He smiles. "Tell me about this illness. What are the stages you mentioned?"

I explain.

"Does it come from the forest here?"

"I don't think so, but there are more plants and animals in places like this that are near the equatorial belt. That's why I thought there might be a useful compound here."

He listens as I explain that my mother is in a London hospital, wasting away. Of course, I don't explain that that's many years in the future. He's as sympathetic to me as to the lady whose father he helped.

I soon realise I really like him.

*

At four p.m., Ramo closes the hut door, and says, "Time to work on your mother's mystery illness, Dori." He pulls out a notepad, asks me tons of questions, and makes a lot of notes. Then he points to one jar after another, and explains that this plant it contains reduces nausea, or that one can reduce bone distortion, or another may bring my mother out of her coma. "But without knowing the origin of the disease, it's more difficult. It's not like when we pick dock leaves to soothe nettle rash. Without more information, all I can do is treat the symptoms."

We talk more and he writes more notes. At last he says, "I must go to my quarters soon, but I'll take you to the village first. They'll find a place for you to stay while I investigate this. Come."

"You don't live in the village?" I ask, as he locks the door.

"No, I stay in the forest with the other *vegetalistas*. I studied in Rio for my undergraduate degree, and then did a medical and biochemistry course at the University of Buenos Aires." He picks up a rucksack and shrugs it onto one shoulder. "Now I study with Mateo and his *vegetalistas*. I want to pick up their knowledge of local plants and herbs. If I can discover plant medicines which will benefit everyone, both here and where you live, it would be a good source of income for the tribes. Everyone wins." He beckons. "This way."

We strike off through the rainforest again.

At the village I'm greeted with mixed levels of enthusiasm. The children are fascinated and cluster around me. The adults are less inclined to welcome me, but the headman, Ramo's father, offers me a spare hut to stay in.

It takes just a few days for us to fall into a routine. I help Ramo to treat the injured and sick among his tribe till four o'clock or so, then work with him and the various compounds he has access to for the cure, before we retire to our respective dwelling-places.

A few days later, while I help Ramo treat a child with a snake bite, a man enters the hut.

Ramo introduces us. "This is Mateo, the leader of the *vegetalistas* I study with. And this is Dori, my new assistant."

Mateo frowns. "So. The stories are true," he hisses. "You *are* working with a woman. That will compromise your purity, for sure."

Ramo smiles in an amused way. "It doesn't have to."

"Be careful, then, Ramo. You are the best of us, and you bring with you much knowledge of diseases, and we help you with cures known among the tribes." Mateo stares at me for his next comment. "The villagers are all afraid of this female shaman, who arrived as naked as a newborn, and brought with her a false quest." Mateo's face is closed and dark with gathering threat, like a cloud that promises a thunderstorm. Then he leaves the treatment hut.

Later, when all the patients have left, I ask, "What did Mateo mean about me compromising your purity?"

Ramo explains that as he has become a *vegetalista* he is subject to a regime of purification, which includes not eating certain foods, and avoiding sex.

I feel something inside me wither. *Probably just hope,* I tell myself. Ramo hasn't given me any reason to think he likes me as a woman.

I get up to return to the village, but Ramo captures my hand. "Mateo has some grounds for his comment," he says. "I do like you. A lot."

"I like you too, Ramo," I say, "but won't you get in trouble –?"

And then he kisses me. I like that a lot too.

"Ah, Dori," he says, "I've been wrestling with my feelings for you ever since you came here."

"Me too," I breathe, before our lips meet again.

*

And that's how it started.

Every day we work on the cure for most of those precious couple of hours, but spend the last half-hour or so in each other's arms. Luckily, nobody in the village will intrude into Ramo's research time. And he locks the door.

"Do you seriously intend to spend the rest of your life working with these *vegetalista* men, Ramo?" I ask one afternoon, as he strokes my hair. We lie side by side on the floor.

"That was the intention originally," he says. "But now – I don't know. I want to learn their knowledge, but I want to be with you, too. I am torn."

And then I know. *It's time to tell him.* I don't think twice about it but jump into an explanation, though not about the time travel – not yet. "You could always come with me if things get too sticky here."

"To London?" he asks. "That never occurred to me."

And over the next few weeks the research yields dividends. We have a list of compounds to mitigate the effects of the disease, and are now looking at its cause too.

"I'd know where to look better if we had a sample," Ramo says one afternoon.

Unease grabs my heart. "I know, Ramo, but it's too dangerous to handle samples, even if they were available here. You'd need specialist protection – a special suit and so on. My mother *had* all that protection – and now she's in a coma, in an isolation tent. I can't even touch her. They don't know how she became contaminated."

"What's an isolation tent?" he asks. "I don't remember that from my studies."

I've slipped up, I realise. *They weren't invented till the 1970s.*

I sigh, and decide there's nothing for it but to tell him I'm from the future. "Ramo, there's something I need to tell you," I begin.

But he's already worked it out. "I'd never heard of Morocco Fever until you mentioned it. Are you really even from this planet?"

"New diseases appear all the time," I say, "but this one's different. It appeared in Morocco, but came from a different timeline. I've been there – it's terrible. A criminal enabled sick people to bring it to our timeline and spread it."

"But how does anyone go from one timeline to another?"

I can see now that I've opened a can of worms, and feel a twinge of sympathy for Alia. I remember my hostility to her in the coffee bar. "I had to learn to time-trip to come here," I tell

47

him. "It's a bumpier ride than usual to cross the timelines, but it's the same technique as travelling to a different place or time."

He stares at me. "I've never met anyone from the future before."

"Me neither, until I met Alia." And I explain about the Caxtan Temporals, and Alia's quest for knowledge, and where my mother's illness fits into it.

He sits in silence as he assimilates it all. He's very quiet for the rest of the afternoon, just holding me.

"What's the matter?" I ask.

"I understand that you need to go back to your future in London. You'll leave me behind."

"I won't," I say. "I've no intention of leaving you behind. I've planned for you to come with me."

"But how? I can't do that – that tripping thing you talked about."

"But I can." I hope I'm right. "When Alia took me with her to the timeline where Morocco fever originated, she held my hand the whole time. I could do the same with you." I'm half-sure it'll work, but I don't tell him that.

His brown eyes gaze at me. "And who will look after the health of the tribe?"

I see that will be a problem for them. But I review Mateo's attitude towards me and realise I need to shape my vague plan into a sharper outline. It's essential to avoid difficulties with the other *vegetalistas*, and I sense that their hostility to me grows daily.

*

I've been here nearly two months when I realise I've missed a period. *Should I tell Ramo?* I decide to wait till I'm sure, and of course, we can't go until the cure's ready. I imagine giving birth here, in the rainforest, and shudder, though I know Ramo will be beside me.

I know I can't take a physical list of cure ingredients with me, so I make a huge effort to memorise them, and as much of the work we've done as possible.

It's my seventy-first day in the rainforest when I decide it's time to tell Ramo he's going to be a father. By this time, there's no mistaking the fact that my waistline has increased. I won't be able to wear the shorts Ramo lent me much longer.

It's not long before he notices, as he caresses me.

"I've been meaning to tell you about that," I say. "I think I'm pregnant."

His reaction isn't quite what I expect. "Then we must think about carrying out your plan before long. I have noticed that Mateo's attitude towards me has changed recently, and I must protect you – and now, the baby."

"I'm sure Mateo disapproves of your friendship with me," I say. I deliberately hold back from saying how I really perceive Mateo's feelings towards me.

Ramo doesn't. "He hates you," he says. "He'll hate you even more if you're pregnant."

"Why? Why is he so bitter? I thought the *vegetalistas* were meant to be healers in the community."

"His tribe was slaughtered when he was just a kid, he says by Europeans from a mining company. He views Europe as a force for evil. The *vegetalistas* found him, took him in, and raised him, but he certainly sees the world differently from most of us. He's not particularly happy about the source of my knowledge, despite some of it dove-tailing quite neatly with the *vegetalismo*, the tenets of his kind of shamanism. If necessary, you should leave, to save yourself. I'm afraid for what he might do if he found out about the baby. If we're going together, we should leave soon, and quietly."

*

Back in my hut, I wondered what Ramo classified as 'soon'. *Should we leave tomorrow? Should we stay a few more days? How long will we be safe?*

The next morning I go to Ramo's hut before the villagers queue up for his services. He has the only key, so I wait for him to arrive.

Apart from a "Good morning, Dori," he says nothing until we're inside. Then he asks "Would you like a coffee to start?"

Although it's my morning habit, I feel an extreme reluctance to drink coffee. "I might skip that today," I say. "I don't really feel like it."

"Oh. Oh, I see. Have you had breakfast?"

I shake my head. "I don't feel like that either." The truth is, I feel quite queasy.

"I think we should go as soon as we can," Ramo says. "I don't feel safe now. I think the other *vegetalistas* know."

"We should go today," I agree. "But how would they *know*?"

"Villagers may have noticed and told them about you. It only takes a sister or father to spot something different about someone, and the vine of grapes will swing into action here."

"The grapevine," I murmur, and snap my fingers. "I was sick last night when I got back."

"And you have the start of a bump," he sighs. "Mateo's no fool. He'll put two and two together and make half a dozen. And be ready to act."

The first of the sick and injured villagers waits as Ramo opens the door. A mother with a poorly baby stands waiting. I wonder if she's overheard what we said, but reassure myself that we spoke in English.

The mother smiles at me, and although I smile back, I wonder whether hers was the smile of a woman for another woman's pregnancy, or simply because she knows I work with Ramo. *Stop that!* I tell myself. *That way lies paranoia.*

That mother is the first of a stream of patients that day. They come in twos and threes, and not just from Ramo's village. But around mid-afternoon, the stream dries up, and Ramo says he'd like to get a breath of fresh air. He holds my hand briefly, then steps away towards the village. I watch him go with misgivings, then go back into the hut, in case anyone else comes while he's out. I have enough of the language to talk to the tribespeople now when needful, and have acquired enough knowledge to help in some of the simpler cases.

And it's while I wait that I see myself.

There are no patients, and I amuse myself by reciting the list of ingredients Ramo and I have found for the cure. As I do so, I see my reflection appear in the mirror. Stunned, I observe myself glance around the hut from the threshold, then disappear.

What the -?

Why would I do that? And did I come from the past or the future? The question niggles at me, but I know there has to be an answer, and that it's important.

At length Ramo returns, and his hands aren't empty. "I've got a new ingredient," he says. He's excited, and shows me a root. It's now research time, and we grate the root and make love while the roots boil.

Afterwards, I ask Ramo what the plant the root came from is called, as he adds the new ingredient to the brew we concocted two days before and re-boil the whole panful.

"I'll write it down for you," he promises. "I don't know the Latin name, or even if it has one. But I remembered it this morning and wondered if it would have the right properties to be the final ingredient of the cure." He tears a sheet of paper out of his notebook and writes on it. "I looked it up back at my quarters, and it does. So I went and got some."

"Fantastic! Ramo, thank you so much!"

"We'll take it with us –"

"Oh, Ramo, we can't!" I explain about not being able to take anything, including clothes, with us. "That's why I arrived naked."

He looks so crestfallen that I *have* to reassure him…

*

"We must go now," Ramo whispers, about twenty minutes later. "Is there anything you need to take with you?"

"Only you, and that piece of paper with the name on it."

"I thought you said you couldn't take anything at all with you?"

"I need to memorize the name before we go. I know all the other plant names."

"I'll write it on your hand," he offers.

"I'm not even sure that would work – and in any case, what if –"

"That's not going to happen," he says. "I'll be with you."

We peer out of the window to see if anyone's watching us. All appears clear.

But we only have vision in one direction from inside the hut. Ramo goes to the door. He opens it a crack, squints through the gap, then pulls the door open wider. "I think it's OK," he says, and steps through.

I follow him out into the clearing. We stand there a moment, not touching each other.

It's then that I see Ramo jerk as if under an impact.

As he collapses beside me I jump back. My first aid training from my job takes over by reflex. I feel for his pulse; it's there, but chaotic. *He's in shock.* I turn him onto his side to look for the cause, and put him into the recovery position.

A tiny dart protrudes from his back. Although no shaman, I know better than to touch it. A single drop of blood oozes from it. There isn't much time. I step over him, kneel and bend my face to his. His pupils are dilated; the poison paralyses his lungs. He tries to speak, but can only mouth the words to me: *I love you.* He shudders as his muscles tense in a seizure, then his whole body goes limp.

His pulse stills. Sorrow drowns me as the stream of blood widens to mimic the Amazon.

But there's no time for grief. The other *vegetalistas* must be close by. I must flee through the rainforest for my life. And perhaps he wasn't just killed for being my lover. *He was so close to finding the cure for Morocco Fever...*my *quest has got my lover killed.*

The dart took him from behind. *Now the other* vegetalistas *will come after me.* It's what I fear most.

I don't have Ramo's extensive knowledge of the jungle and its dangers, just my ability to trip, honed through my many attempts to get here. *That's my way out.* The Caxtan Temporals' secrecy must apply wherever I go; but the tribe are a mile away, and some of them already think I'm a female shaman practising magic on the quiet. *No doubt that's Mateo's doing.* The other *vegetalistas* are a different matter. *I need to leave this place.* I set off through the forest.

Seconds later I trip over a tree-root jutting out of the ground and find myself on the rainforest floor. A scrape on my shin oozes blood; I nurse my sore toe where the nail has broken off below the quick. *Finding that will point to me, and they'll follow my blood trail. There's nothing to keep me here now.*

I scramble upright, only to confront the largest snake I've ever seen, dangling from a low bough. It draws back its head to strike and opens its mouth. Its tongue flickers.

Behind it, one of the *vegetalistas* wears a vicious grin.

I step back and raise my hands to protect my face. Then I back away, inch by inch.

A man's harsh voice whips my head around. "You tempted Ramo to give up his purification regime with your false quest, Dori." It's Mateo. "He was the best of us, but is no longer one of us. Now *you* will die and join him."

There's only one way to escape.

But before I can leave, there's something I must do. I still need the name of the final plant, and though he wrote it down, the piece of paper is back at the surgery. Because we were leaving together, I haven't brought it with me. We both assumed he'd be with me in the future.

My first jump is from the forest back to the surgery. I see the look of astonishment on Mateo's face as I fade from his view; then the currents of time pluck me out of the *vegetalistas'* grip. Seconds later I stand on the threshold of the hut. I look into it and catch sight of myself in Ramo's mother's mirror. I notice myself sitting alone in the hut, leaning one arm on the worktop.

And of course, now I understand what I saw earlier in the afternoon.

I've arrived too early.

I've always tripped out in the open, so I figure that's a pre-requisite for it. So I go outside, knowing I'll be safe for a few moments. And there I trip a second time, forwards in time by a couple of hours.

I hang suspended in a void between realities for what seems like an eternity. As soon as my feet touch solid ground again, I hurry back into the hut.

I'm too late. The precious brew is smeared all over the worktop, the glass vessels smashed. Their fragments cover the worktop and floor. Worse still, all Ramo's other jars and ointments and plant samples are broken or torn to shreds as well. *The place is trashed,* I think. *All the ingredients are mixed up. They'll never be any use again.*

I avoid treading on the glass as I make my way over to the worktop.

The paper's there, ripped into irregular shapes. I pick up the pieces and lay them together. They make a word that sounds familiar. I write it on the palm of my hand in biro: 'gabiquat'. Then I hurry outside again as darkness gathers in the rainforest. My mind repeats a chant of the name to memorise it.

But I must abandon that to leave, or its distraction will prevent me from going. In my mind's eye I build a picture of the alley where I left my clothes.

The giant leaves of the trees become massive mirrors that glitter around me; the sun's light flares in them as their lobes separate, only to blast through me. But the sensation of tumbling and vertigo is less, until the wind leans in to pluck me from my surroundings.

I'm sure this is my last trip. And with one great leap I wrench myself out of the 1950s rainforest and fall back into a dim dawn in twenty-first century Britain.

*

And when I look down at my arm, the biro marks have gone.

What was the bloody name of that plant? Panic hits me as I try to remember. *Gabi-something.*

I can't remember. I only know the other ingredients.

I look around the alley. My clothes aren't there.

I've arrived back at the place I left from; it matches my memory. *Someone's found them.* "Shit!"

So I creep between patches of shadow to get home. It's a chilly morning. When I finally stumbled into my kitchen, I shiver as I bang on the door for Alia to let me in. And once inside, I blurt out to Alia my one thought: "Am I too late to see my mother alive again?"

"I saw Dani yesterday," Alia says. "She still has a few hours. She should still make it, if you have anything for her."

I stare at her as I realise she doesn't know what I've discovered. "I'm sorry – I couldn't bring back a fully-developed cure. I barely escaped with my life, and a friend died because of me."

"No cure?"

"Yes – maybe. But untested. The tribes in Africa were resettled into slums fifteen years ago. There was no-one to ask there. But I lived with one of the last two Amazonian rainforest tribes for a couple of months – back in the 1950s." I slump into a seat. "I left in a hurry. Ramo hadn't quite found the cure, though he had symptom relievers, and a promising candidate for the thing that would bind it all together and deal with the infection itself." For a moment I raise my hand as if to check it. Then I remember that the biro marks have faded. "All I have is a list of ingredients I learned by heart, though it will take years of research and experimentation to find the correct combination of them and dose to counteract the virus." And I explain about the final ingredient we'd found, and that I can't remember what its name is.

Alia lifts her shoulders, then lets them drop. "We've done all we can for now, then," she mutters, and her voice has a hollow twang. "You'd better tell me everything. For a start, how you got pregnant!"

"The usual way," I huff. She's helped herself to my clothes, and I'm not pleased about it. *They'll probably end up being abandoned somewhere, or get lost in another timestream.* "Now can we *please* go to the hospital so I can see my mother? I'll tell you what happened on the way."

"Of course." I see and hear her disappointment. "At least you learned to control your trips."

"Yes," I say. "It became easier when I remembered what you said about visualising where you wanted to go."

"And – the baby?"

"Ramo's – my *vegetalista* friend. He helped me. We – fell in love."

Alia nods as if she understands perfectly. "Get some clothes on. I'll call a taxi. At least we'll arrive fully clothed! No more mess-ups, Dori."

"What d'you mean?"

"The police found your clothes after you tripped. You're listed as missing."

"You could have brought them home."

"The police arrived just after you left. They found your clothes and I just about got back here without anyone seeing me. Thank you for trusting me with your keys, though."

I grunt an acknowledgement as I struggle into a t-shirt and trousers that strain across my waist. I feel sweaty, but there's no time for a shower. The taxi races us to hospital.

Yet despite the mad rush, I feel myself slowing down inside, as if my own internal clock is losing time. The sense of urgency which thrust me back and forth in time, like seaborne driftwood, is gone. The end is near but I feel calm. It may be exhaustion, but I don't think so. The spring inside me has wound down. *Little touches me,* I reason, *because my grief blocks my ability to take it in. I'm awake in a nightmare, but unable to wake fully, though no-one around me is asleep.*

But Alia tucks my arm through hers and steers me down the white corridor. I remember everything in slow motion. Through the isolation tent I can see that my mother's cheeks are gaunt, yellow and sunken; a month ago they were rounded and rosy.

"It's jaundice," the nurse explains. "We've made her comfortable. I'm sorry. There's nothing else to be done now."

I sink into a chair. At least I've seen her before she dies. My eyes close…

*

A crocodile has my arm in its mouth. It shakes it back and forth and calls my name at the same time. *Odd. I'm pretty sure crocodiles in the rainforest don't speak.*

"Wake up, Dori!"

I open my eyes. Alia kneels by my chair, hand on my arm. I feel refreshed, but calm.

"She's come round – the last stage. I can buy her more time, so she can find the cure, but we must hurry. And I need that list of ingredients." She grips my arm. "Remember when we met? I thought I'd made contact with your mother."

I remember her confusion amidst the coffee cups, and nod.

"*My* records showed me Dani, an attractive young woman in her late twenties. And a daughter, Dori, born a few months later, who grows up to become a physicist and carry out research into time travel. She invents a teleportation system which becomes the basis of the Caxtan Temporals' work, and meanwhile Dani finds the cure for Morocco Fever." She pauses for a moment. "I couldn't understand the discrepancies between the dates. And there was nothing in those records to show that you – as you are now – ever lived."

"I have a National Insurance number," I point out.

She nods, and smiles as if she's gained confidence. "You love your mother, don't you?"

"Of course. Can you doubt that? I've just been halfway around the world to get a cure for her."

"So – you'd take *any* route to help her survive?"

I nod. "Within reason."

"Trust me?"

She's been right about everything. I nod, though I'm not sure I'd have called it trust.

She smiles. "Dori, I need your body. Or rather, Dani does."

"Eh? What's my body got to do with this?" A movement within the plastic shrouds distracts me momentarily. My mother's hand, lifted in a salute.

"You must make one last trip."

"In here? I thought we always needed to be outside –"

"Indoors is fine for inter-body tripping." Alia smiled. "I'm so proud of you, Dori. You've gained enough control to focus your aim, and you already know you can travel to places as well as different times. I'll help Dani make the switch at the same time."

"Where am I going?" I demand.

"Into that baby in your own womb."

"*What?* You want *me* to displace my own child?"

"You won't have to displace her. You'll grow together – form a dual intellect and personality. But Dani's fading fast. We have just minutes before she goes."

How do I make such a decision? I weigh everything Alia said. Within me a conviction grows, and with it a surge of confidence. This *is* the only way.

I take the phone out of my handbag and give it to her. "Let's record the list of ingredients on the voice recorder on this. Then you can have it. I guess I won't be needing it for a few years."

Alia nods approval. "Great idea."

When we've finished, I draw in a deep breath. "I'm ready."

*

We float, aware of nothing but our safety. The warm liquid around us pulses in time with our heartbeat. A faint view of the outside world reaches us through the red mist of skin.

We are never sure how long we float like this. But at last we yawn, stretch, tumble over, and press our head downwards. Then a journey, perhaps the first of many. Who knows where we will go?

The tunnel squeezes us forward. The sensation isn't unpleasant, just new. Every pulse caresses our skin. We wait. A squeeze. We wait. The journey is long but we have no fear. We will arrive. Certainty grows with every pulse and squeeze. The red mist is still there, but ahead we perceive a brighter circle. Red lines wriggle and intertwine across the mist, pulse as the rhythm suffuses every part of our existence.

The mist grows paler. Squeeze. Wait. Paler. Squeeze. Wait. We gather ourselves up, waiting for the final push. It comes in a rush. We're catapulted from the safety of the tunnel around us, ready to begin life's journey again.

Something touches us. We draw our first breath and scream.

It is a scream of pure triumph.

She... is also available from Amazon as a Kindle e-book.

For further information about the universe of *The Stallion* and *Floodtide*, including starmaps, a timeline, and other forthcoming publications by this author, visit: www.Zarduth.com.

Look out for Helen Claire Gould's next novel, *The Zarduth Imperative: Discovery.*

ABOUT THE AUTHOR

Helen Claire Gould has been writing since her teens, having read her first two Science Fiction novels at the age of nine. At the Peterborough SF Club, where she met her husband, she contributed to the club fanzine *A Change of Zinery*. After suffering some miscarriages in 1992 she began writing for therapeutic reasons, joining Orbiters (SF postal writing workshops) and setting up the Peterborough Science Fiction Writers' Group. She edited two small press collections of short fiction, *Shadows on a Broken Wall* and *Mother Milk, Father Flywheel*, organised a weekend workshop on writing for comics, and had book reviews published in the BSFA review magazine, *Vector*.

Returning to full-time education in 1995, Helen graduated in Geology and Planetary science in 2000, teaching Geology and Creative Writing evening classes, and editing further collections of short fiction by her Creative Writing students. In 2013 she organised and ran a series of writers' workshops for the Peterborough Arts Festival.

Floodtide was Helen's first published novel, and was set in her own fictional universe. *The Stallion* is an ecological fantasy loosely based in that universe. *She...* is a collection of original short stories, not based in that universe, with a background theme of fertility and motherhood.